For Sunny & Story.

Thanks to James, Taylor, Lydia, Rosa, Jill, Aaron, Jessixa, Puppy, and Mom.

Library of Congress Cataloging-in-Publication Data available.

ISBN 978-1-7972-0689-9

Manufactured in China.

MIX
Paper | Supporting responsible forestry
FSC™ C008047
FSC
www.fsc.org

Design by Lydia Ortiz & Jill Turney.
Typeset in Darin's Hand.
The illustrations in this book were rendered in mixed media.

10 9 8 7 6 5 4 3 2 1

Chronicle Books LLC
680 Second Street
San Francisco, California 94107
www.chroniclekids.com

Dog & Hat
and the
Lunar Eclipse Picnic

BOOK № 2

By Darin Shuler

chronicle books · san francisco

1

Ant's Dream

ACROSS THE SKY, ON THAT
SHINING MOON, LIVE OUR COUSINS,
THE MOON ANTS . . .

"SO THEY CLIMBED TO THE TOP OF A TALL TOWER WHERE MOON MAGIC NEVER FADES,

THE HOME OF A BUNNY BORN OF DREAMS."

"THE ANTS MARCHED OUT THE WINDOW

TO THE TIP OF THE SPIRE."

"IT IS SAID THAT THE MOON ANTS ARE LIKE THEIR EARTH COUSINS . . .

EXCEPT THEY HAVE DREAMY POWERS FROM EATING MOON CRUMBS AND SOAKING IN MOONLIGHT."

"ON VERY SPECIAL MOON OCCASIONS, A CHAIN OF MOON ANTS RETURN TO THE PRECISE PLACE THEY LEFT OUR PLANET . . ."

TO CELEBRATE WITH THEIR COUSINS . . .

"AND SHOW THEM THE MOON'S DREAMY MAGIC!"

2

A Very Special
Moon Occasion

15

3

An Impossible
Adventure

BUT WHY?!

WHO MADE UP THESE RULES?

THE WORLD HAS RULES! THAT'S THE WAY IT IS, OR IT WOULDN'T BE THAT WAY.

HEY, LOOK OVER THERE! THAT GUY COMING FROM THE BATHROOM DIDN'T WASH HIS HANDS!

HALT

WHERE? THAT'S NOT ALLOWED!

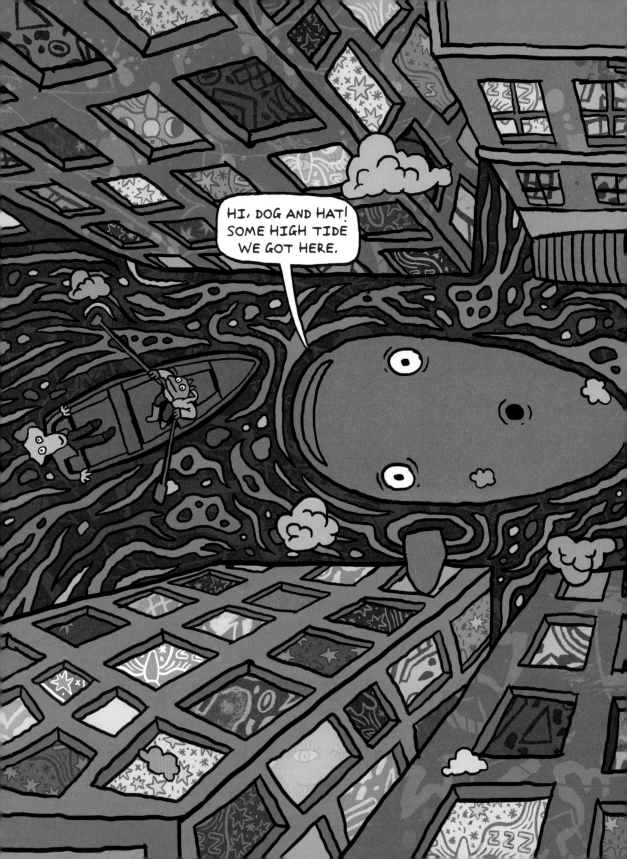

FLOOP

55

5

Let the Moon Festivities Begin!

THERE WERE DINOSAUR RACES, MOON MAZES, PAINTED FACES, MOON CRUMB-EATING CONTESTS, AND, UM, WELL, LIKE A DREAM, I CAN'T REMEMBER IT ALL.

6

Hat's Dream

FOR THE FIRST TIME IN HIS LIFE, HAT BREAKS THE RULES. ONE NIGHT HE SNEAKS OUT OF THE HATBOX...

50,000 PIECES

AND CATCHES A BUS TO THE BIG CITY.

Total Eclipse

REMEMBER, DEAR READER, THAT YOU ALWAYS WANT TO GET PERMISSION BEFORE TICKLING A BUDDY.

8

Friendship

BUT DOG IS ALREADY DREAMING.
What's cookin'?
Mama's Crispy Peanut Butter MOON BALLS
serves 4 doz.
• combine 2 cups crunchy peanut butter w/1 stick unsalted butter & 1 tsp. vanilla
• add 2 cups powdered sugar
• stir in 2 cups crispy rice cereal. use your hands!
+1 cup graham cracker crumbs (optional)
• shape into 1-inch balls; refrigerate for 30 mins on lined baking sheet.
• melt 16 oz. chocolate candy coating
• dip balls into chocolate; don't use your hands!
• set on sheet; add sprinkles
• done when chocolate coating is firm
KRISPY CRUNCH
PB
24
LIKE THIS, MAMA?
PERFECT, DOGGY!